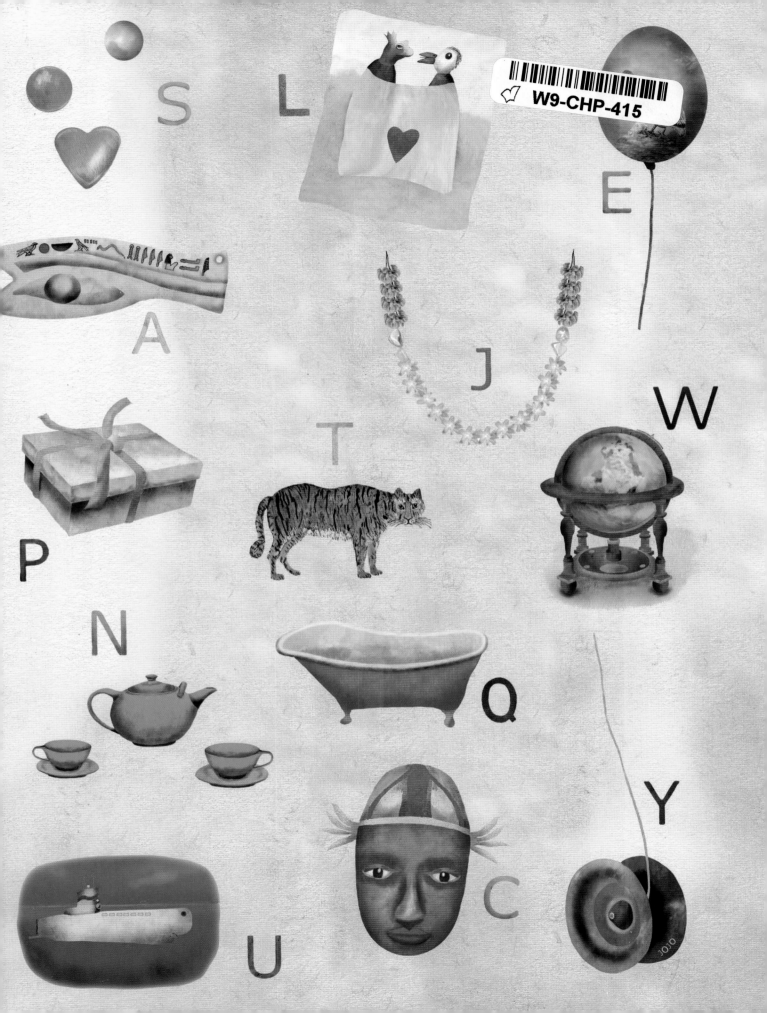

First published in the United States, Great Britain, Canada, Australia, and New Zealand
in 2015 by NorthSouth Books, Inc., an imprint of NordSüd Verlag AG, CH-8005 Zürich,
Switzerland.

Distributed in the United States by NorthSouth Books Inc., New York 10016.
Library of Congress Cataloging-in-Publication Data is available.
ISBN: 978-0-7358-4198-7
Printed in China by Leo Paper Products Ltd., Heshan, Guangdong, October 2014.

1 3 5 7 9 • 10 8 6 4 2
www.northsouth.com

Willy Puchner

The ABC of Fantastic Princes

North South

Prince Willoughby has invited twenty-five unmarried princes from all over the world to attend a fabulous ball. Before the ceremony begins the princesses wander around the portrait gallery of the palace to see pictures of the princes they are soon to meet. It's a royal affair!

And now, without further ado, it's time for Red Rabbit—the master of ceremonies—to call upon each of the princes from A to Z.

"Fantastic princes, hear well—describe yourself to our lovely ladies. Tell them your dreams, your amphibious ambitions, your heart's desires.

"Fabulous princesses, listen carefully, and don't rush into any rash decisions! These froggy, toady princes have come from all over the world, and each one is worthy of your attention. Take a good look; but always be courteous, courtly, and considerate. Then if one of them strikes your fancy, grab him, and don't let go!"

I'm Prince Augustus, born in August in Augsburg, Germany. I'm amazingly athletic, articulate, and adorable, although alas and alack I'm alone! I studied art, astronomy, and anthropology. As an added attraction I have an astonishing appetite for apple strudel. My aristocratic ancestors Aunt Agatha and Uncle Arthur performed acrobatics with alligators. I'm after an amiable, attentive Augustine who is amenable to accepting this ancient, antique amulet from Alexandria.

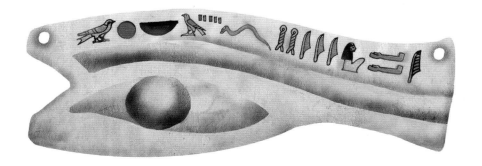

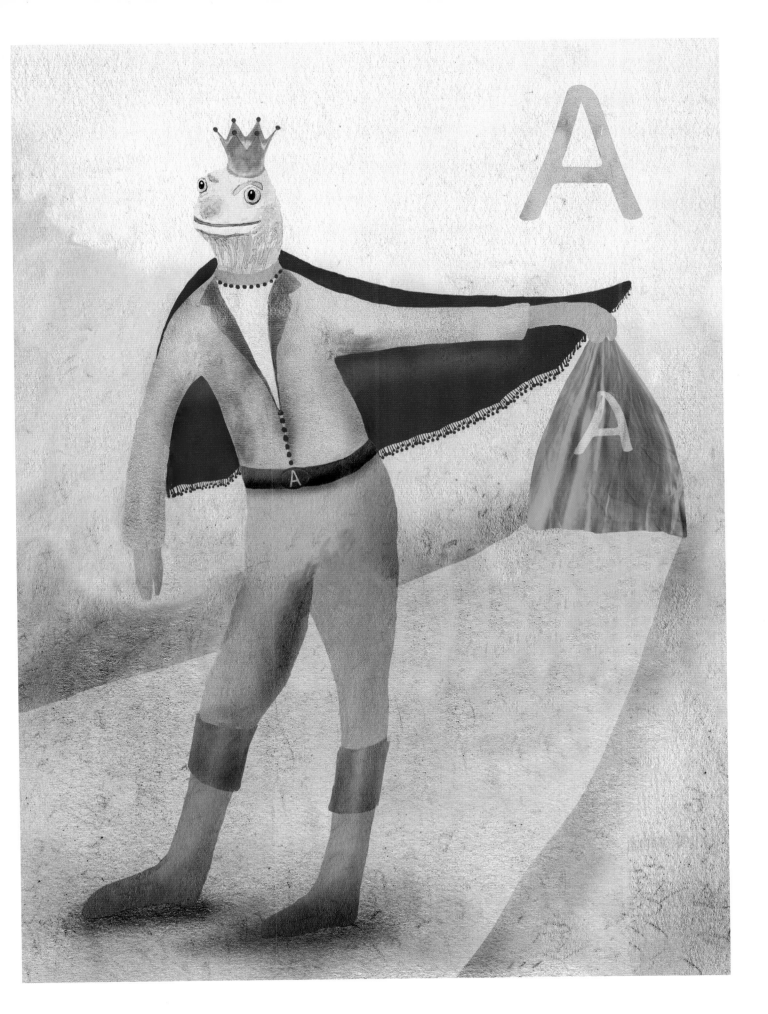

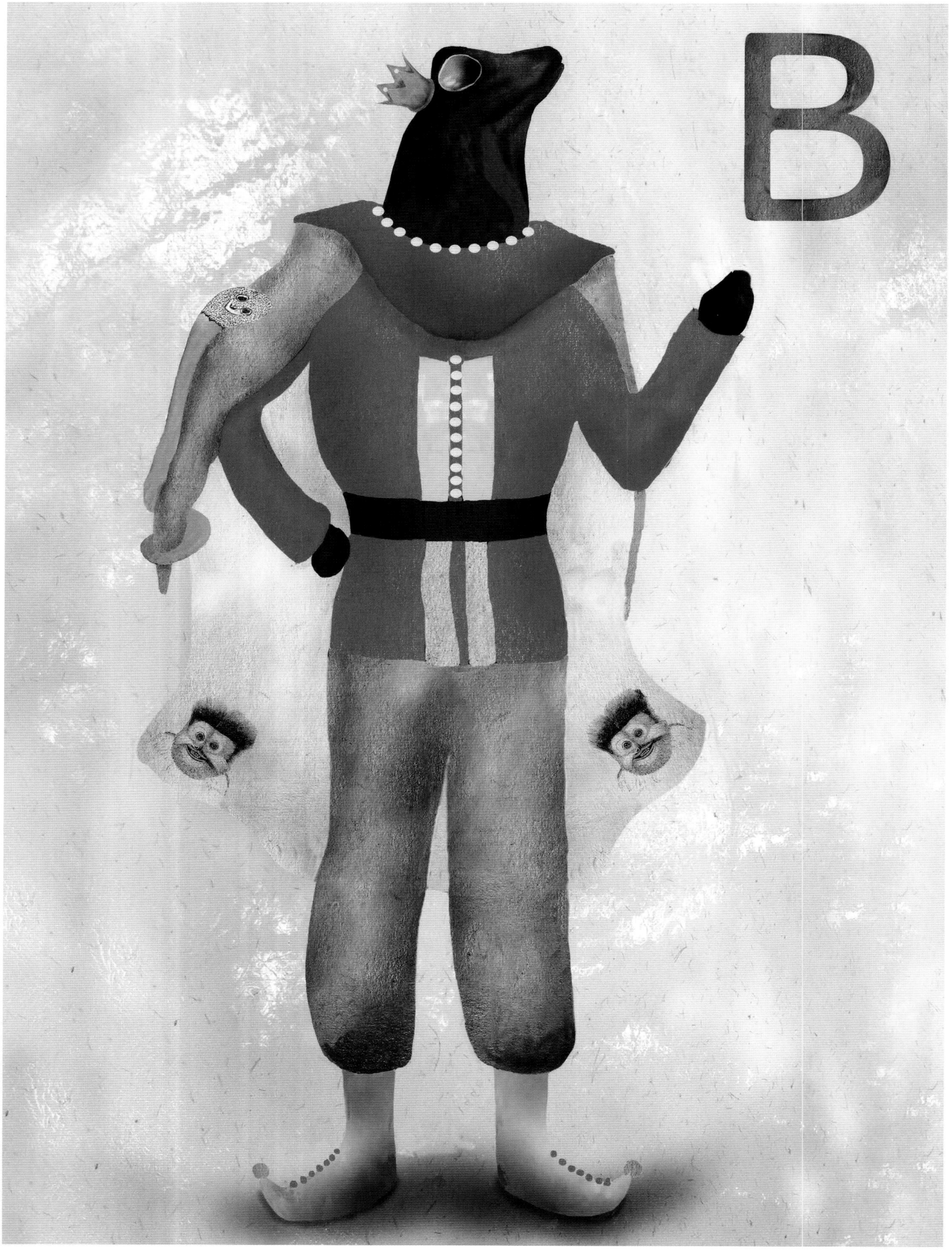
B

I'm Prince Balthazar from Botswana, the boldest, bravest, brightest bigwig in the African bush. I bully boa constrictors, I beat up baboons, and I turn bison into beef. I'm brilliant at baseball, badminton, and billiards. But biochemistry, biophysics, and bio-anything bar biographies of me are unbelievably boring. I brighten at the thought of a benevolent blonde who will bounce our beautiful, babbling babies. I've bought her this beautiful gown for her bridal ball in the bushes behind the baobab.

I am Prince Camillo from
Cambridge in the United Kingdom.
I am clever, charismatic, and as
cool as a cucumber. I'm a composer
who conducts wearing the cap of
a clown. I play the clavichord, the
clarinet, the calliope, and the comb.
In my caravan I keep a cat, a cow,
a cougar, a canary, a crow, and a
crocodile. I cultivate carnations,
chrysanthemums, cacti, and
cupcakes. This coconut carving
from Colombo is for my charming
and courageous Cinderella. I hope
that she has a castle, 'cause mine
is quite crowded.

I am Prince Demetrius from Denmark. I'm dashing, dynamic, dominant, and devastatingly desirable. I'm a doctor, dancer, and deep-thinking dilettante. I deliver discourses, direct my disciples, and demolish their dissertations. I defy the dangers of darkness, devils, disasters, and durians. My dearest diva will have decorations on her dresses, diamonds in her diadem, and darling dimples. I hope she'll delight in these three delicate ducats designed and donated by Demetrius himself.

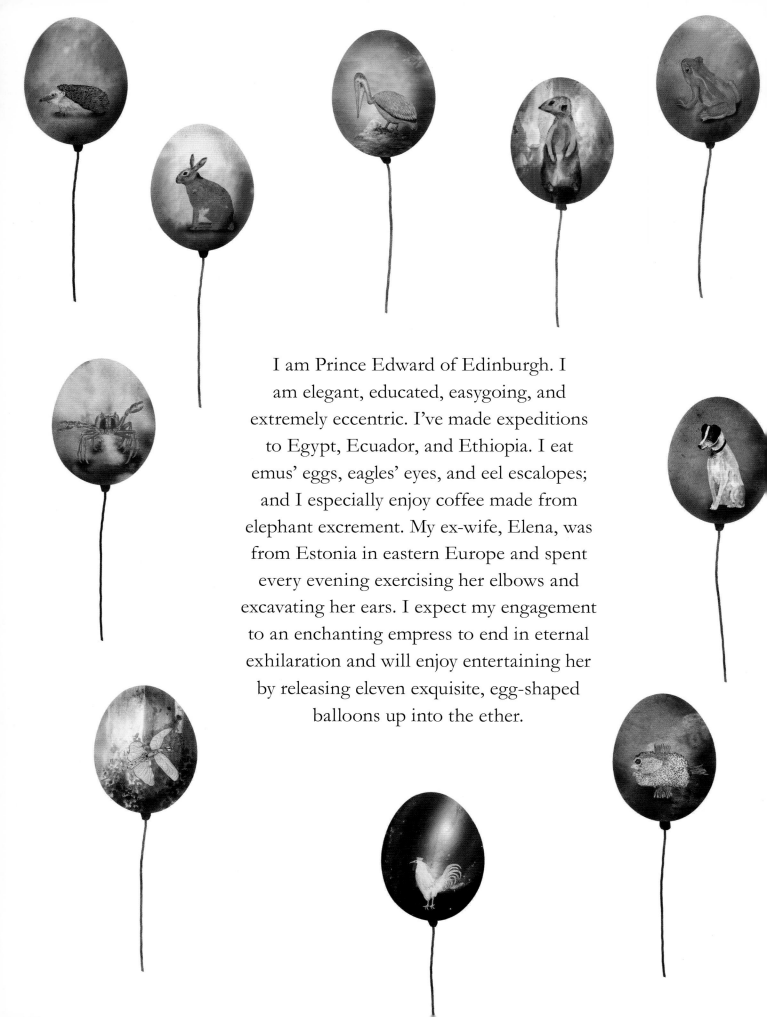

I am Prince Edward of Edinburgh. I am elegant, educated, easygoing, and extremely eccentric. I've made expeditions to Egypt, Ecuador, and Ethiopia. I eat emus' eggs, eagles' eyes, and eel escalopes; and I especially enjoy coffee made from elephant excrement. My ex-wife, Elena, was from Estonia in eastern Europe and spent every evening exercising her elbows and excavating her ears. I expect my engagement to an enchanting empress to end in eternal exhilaration and will enjoy entertaining her by releasing eleven exquisite, egg-shaped balloons up into the ether.

I am Prince Frederick from Ferder Fyr, Norway. I'm frightfully fragile, frail, and fearful. My friends are full of fire and fervor, but I am often as frigid as a flagon of frozen fish fingers. Feast days and festivals, fetes and fairs should be full of festive fun; but I feel faint and frightened of all the fuss and fatuous frolicking. I'd find it more favorable to fly to a faraway, fenced-off fortress, where I can flop by the fireside next to the familiar faces of my family and forbearing friends. I fear I'll never find a fiancée fit to fall in with my flat and foolish fantasies.

G

I'm gorgeous Prince George from Georgia, USA. My great-granddaddy Garth was a gold miner, my granddaddy Grady was a gunsmith, and my daddy Gordon was a guitar-slinging godfather to the greatest gospel-singing group in all Gainesville. My great-uncle Godwin gave me gifts of gum, Gorgonzola, the game of Go, and a guitar. Now I sing in a gospel group. So my girl has got to play Go, sing gospel, and play guitar with the same grace, gusto, and glee as good old me.

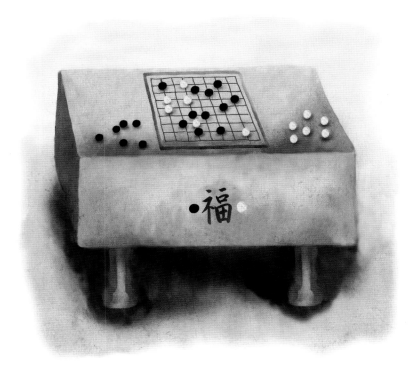

I'm handsome, humorous, and happy
Prince Heinrich from Helsinki.
I hate harshness, hairsplitting, horror
films, hackers, hawkers, and habanero
peppers. I love harmony, healthiness,
humaneness, heroes, holidays, hugs,
high jinks, high fives, high spirits,
hilarity, and halibut. I play the harp,
the horn, the harmonica, the hurdy-
gurdy, and the hi-fi. I have high hopes of
holding to my heart a heroine who'll help
her husband to make history. For her I'd
happily heave a hare out of my hat.

I am Prince Inesh from India. I'm intense and introspective. Isidor is my infant son, intuitive and idealistic. I am not an idiot, and Isidor isn't either. We are interested in our inner selves, our instincts, imagination, inventiveness, and informative innovations such as the Internet, iPods, and iPads. Isidor and I need an intellectual Indira to share our interest in impressionism, immunology, imperialism, and I Ching. Together we will inhabit an idyllic island in the Indian Ocean and inspect the insects, iguanas, ibis, and ichthyosauruses.

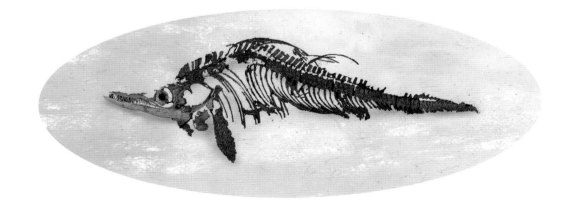

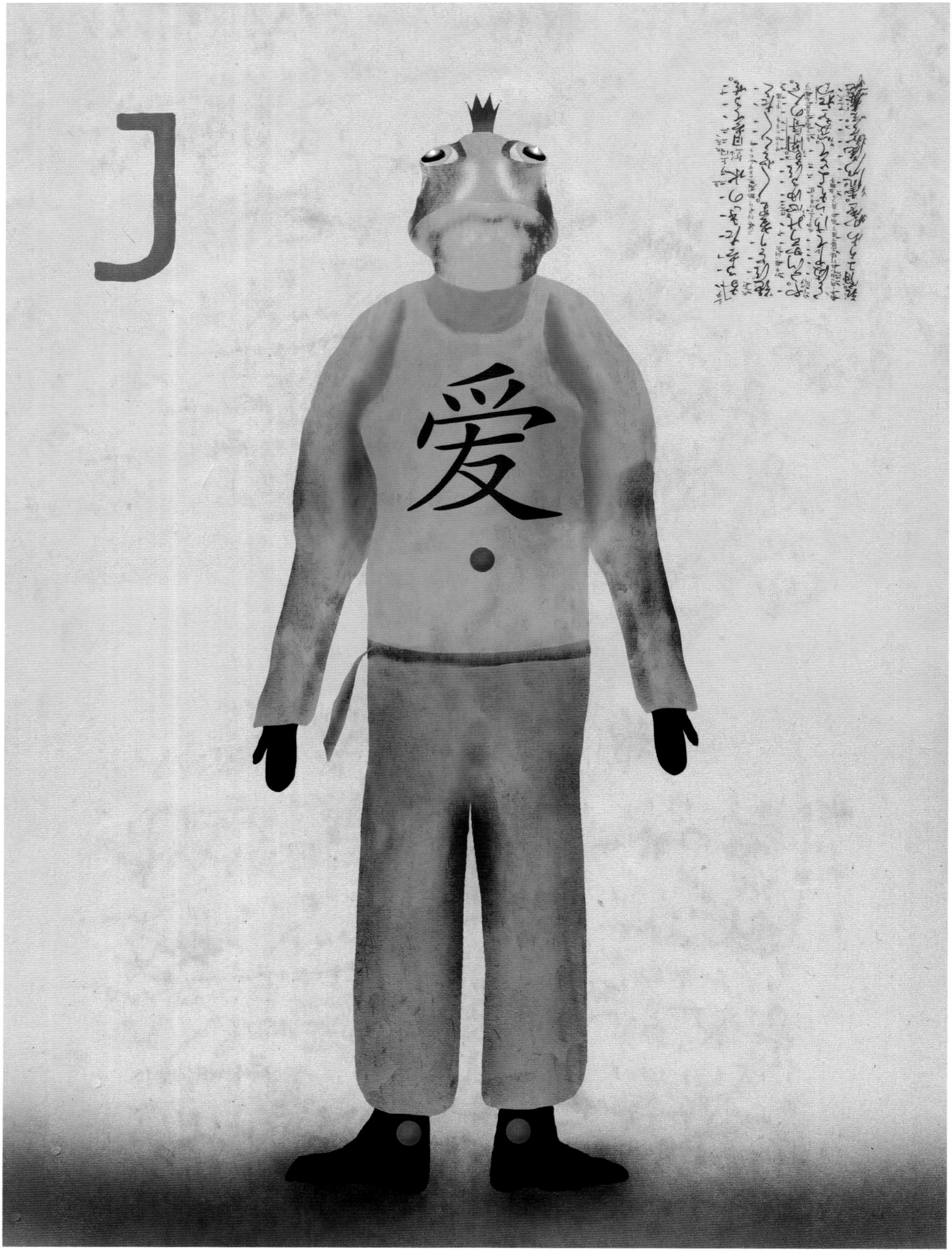
J
爱

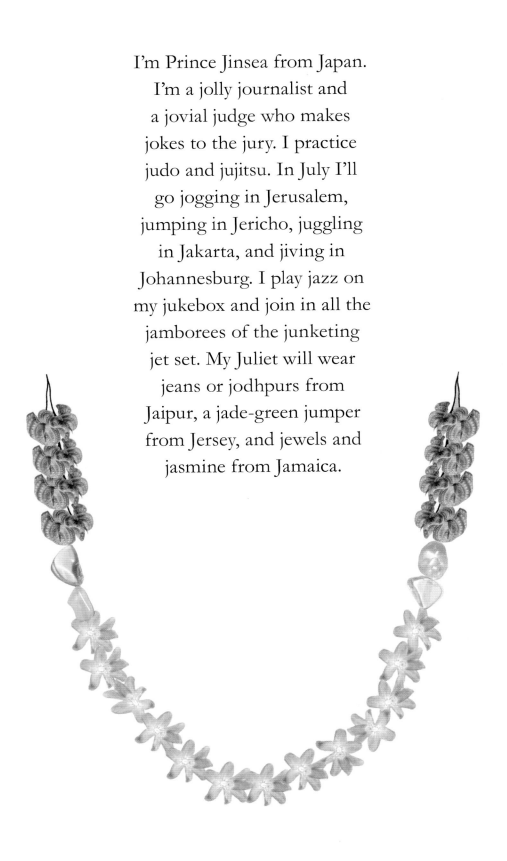

I'm Prince Jinsea from Japan.
I'm a jolly journalist and
a jovial judge who makes
jokes to the jury. I practice
judo and jujitsu. In July I'll
go jogging in Jerusalem,
jumping in Jericho, juggling
in Jakarta, and jiving in
Johannesburg. I play jazz on
my jukebox and join in all the
jamborees of the junketing
jet set. My Juliet will wear
jeans or jodhpurs from
Jaipur, a jade-green jumper
from Jersey, and jewels and
jasmine from Jamaica.

I'm Prince Kaspar from Kalamazoo. In my court I keep kooky kings, kitschy cartoonists, knobbly kneed country cousins, and a knight in knitted knickers. I go kayaking in my kaftan from Kansas to Kentucky, and I ride king-size camel-birds across Kenya, Kuwait, and Kazakhstan, up Kanchenjunga, and down Kilimanjaro. I cuddle koalas and kangaroos, but I keep clear of kraits and king cobras. My queen must be kindhearted and kissable, and we'll keep our keeshonds in a kennel and our kids in kindergarten.

I'm Prince Lahab from Libya. I'm
a little lazy, lax, and lethargic. I like
lolling during lunchtime. I love
luminous, lucent, lambent light.
My library is lit with lamps. There
are lanterns in my lavatory and
lampposts along the line of lime
trees to the left of my labyrinth. If
I lose my way, I lean on a laurel, lick a
lollipop, and let my Labrador lead me
to liberty. I like leeks and lentils, liver
of lamb, loganberries, and lemonade.
I long for a liberal lady with linen
leggings and lacquer shoes who will
make my life lively. We shall live in
a lighthouse and languish as we
read our love letters out loud.

I'm Prince Mojiz from Morocco. I'm
mostly moody, melancholy, and morose.
My mother made me march many miles,
mainly in the middle of a muddy marsh,
to move mountains of muck from the
meadow and master the murky mysteries
of mathematics. My meager moments
of mirth were making music with my
mandolin. I like maracas, munching mince
pies, and manipulating my marionette.
My only friend was a miniature
mouse—more mournful than I.

On Mondays I meditate with monks
and mull over myths, magic, and my
miserable memories. I'd like to marry
a maiden who will make my life more
merry and meaningful.

I'm Prince Nabil, born in Naama, Algeria. I'm a nice but nervous, nature-loving nerd. I live in a niche in no-man's-land, with nothing but narcissi and nasturtiums, nightingales and nightjars, newts and natterjacks. In my nightclothes and my nightcap, I nestle down for a nap at noon. I have nine nephews and nieces: Norman, Norris, Norbert, Nobby, and Nigel, plus Norma, Nellie, Natalie, and Natasha. And my nan will be ninety-nine in November. A naive nun with a nice nose would be nice to know, and at night we'd nibble nuts and nougat.

I am the one-and-only Prince Omar from Oman—outstanding, overbearing, overpowering, and overwhelmingly openhearted if you obey my orders. I own orange and olive trees, and observe owls, ospreys, and ostriches. I also own an opera house. My orchestras only perform opuses by Prince Omar the Omnitalented. I seek an opulently oversize opera singer who will sit on this original, orange-colored Oriental throne, overseeing the ovations openly offered to Prince Omar the Omnipresent, Omniscient, and Omnipotent.

I'm Prince Papik from Paamiut, Greenland. I am a philosopher, philanthropist, and philatelist. I'm peace loving and am prone to prattle on about Portuguese porcelain, Polish potatoes, Paraguayan pineapples, and Peruvian pottery. My palace has a park with pine trees, poplars, and pansies from Pakistan, Panama, and Puerto Rico. I'd prefer to pair with a perfumed princess from Paris who'll provide me with priceless paintings by Picasso. In preparation I've packed her a parcel of pearls, pralines, popcorn, poppadoms, and a picture of Prince Papik posing as Peter Pan.

I am Prince Quentin from Quebec. I am quarrelsome and highly qualified in quantum physics, quantum mechanics, and quantum theory. Quails quack, quiver, and quake when I question them. My quest is for quality, and quibblers quickly quit when I quiz them about quotients, quarks, and quadrillions. I play quarterback for the Quakers, and play quicksteps and quadrilles with a quintet from Quito. My queen must be quietly quiescent and quote quips from *Don Quixote*. As a quid pro quo I shall offer her quiet time in this quaint aquarium from Queensland.

I am Prince Rupert the Revolutionary from Rackwick, Orkney Islands, UK. I am rough and rude, rowdy and raucous, rabidly rebellious, and ravenously rampant. I have raised riots in Russia, Romania, and Rome. I have ranted and raged with Rasputin, robbed the rich with Robin Hood, and rocked and rolled with Ringo Starr. I eat roasted rhino, reindeer ragout, and raw rattlesnake. I'd like to relax with a real-life Red Riding Hood, riding our racehorses round the ruins of ranches I've ransacked. And I shall reward her royally and romantically with this radiantly resplendent red rose.

I'm Prince Simon the Simple from
Sabah in Papua New Guinea. Some
of my subjects say I'm silly and soft
headed because I send salt to the sea,
sand to the Sahara, and snowflakes
to the South Pole. Sometimes I
sing sad songs to sinking sailors,
speak Spanish to spotty spaniels,
stare stonily at stagnant streams,
and slalom slowly down the slippery
slopes in Slovenia. I sleep in a
shirt and shorts, and I snore like a
suffocating sow in a stinky sty.
I shall serenade my smart sweetheart
with my sitar, my saxophone, and my
state-of-the-art stereo system; and as
a special symbol of my sentiments,
I shall surround her with the sweet
softness of my soap bubbles.

I am Prince Tibor from Tabora, Tanzania. I'd like to be tall and tough and terrifying; but I'm timid, tame, and talentless. I tap my timpani out of time, tip my tea all over the tablecloth, and tear my trousers. My tutor tried to teach me to tango, but I tripped over my toes and tore a tendon. I intended to tour Turkey but took the wrong train and was taken to Timbuktu. My truelove will be tender, tactful, and tolerant, and will turn my terrors into triumphs. Thanks to her thoroughness and thoughtfulness I shall thrive thrillingly, topping the tree, turning up trumps, teaching teachers, toppling tyrants, and taming tigers.

I am Prince Ultimus from Ulm, Germany.
I am unbending, unbreakable, unbearable, and
unbeatable. Under me the von Umbachlers
will uphold our unquestionable right to
unseat and uproot any ugly usurpers who
have undermined the undeniable usefulness
of allowing us upper classes to have the upper
hand over the under classes whose only use
is to be underlings to us von Umbachlers.
My uxorial union will be with an upstanding,
upbeat, up-and-coming, up-and-at-'em Ute,
who will understand my urgent undertakings
as we unveil my unsinkable U-boat.

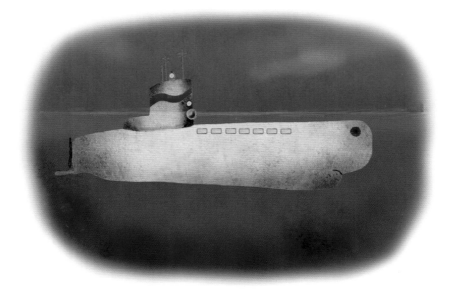

I'm Prince Victor from Vienna.
I am a virtuoso on the viola, violin,
and saxophone. My velvety voice is
valued by visitors from Venezuela
and Verona to Valencia and the
Vatican. I vilify violence, viruses,
venom, and vandalism; but I'll
vote for virtue, vitality, Vermeer,
Vincent van Gogh, veggie burgers,
Vegemite, and vitamins.

My Venus will be voluptuous and
vivacious, and will love this very
valuable violet volume of visionary
verses and verities.

I'm the warmhearted, well-mannered, weary, and woebegone Prince Willoughby of Warsaw. I have wandered the world, worshipped its wonders, and wept at its wickedness. When I witness the worries of the weak and the wiles of the wealthy, I want to work toward wiser ways of living. I love the wild wastes of the wilderness, the whales wallowing in the waves, and the winds waging war on the waters. The woman who will be my wife will wander the world with me, will wonder with me, and will weep with me.

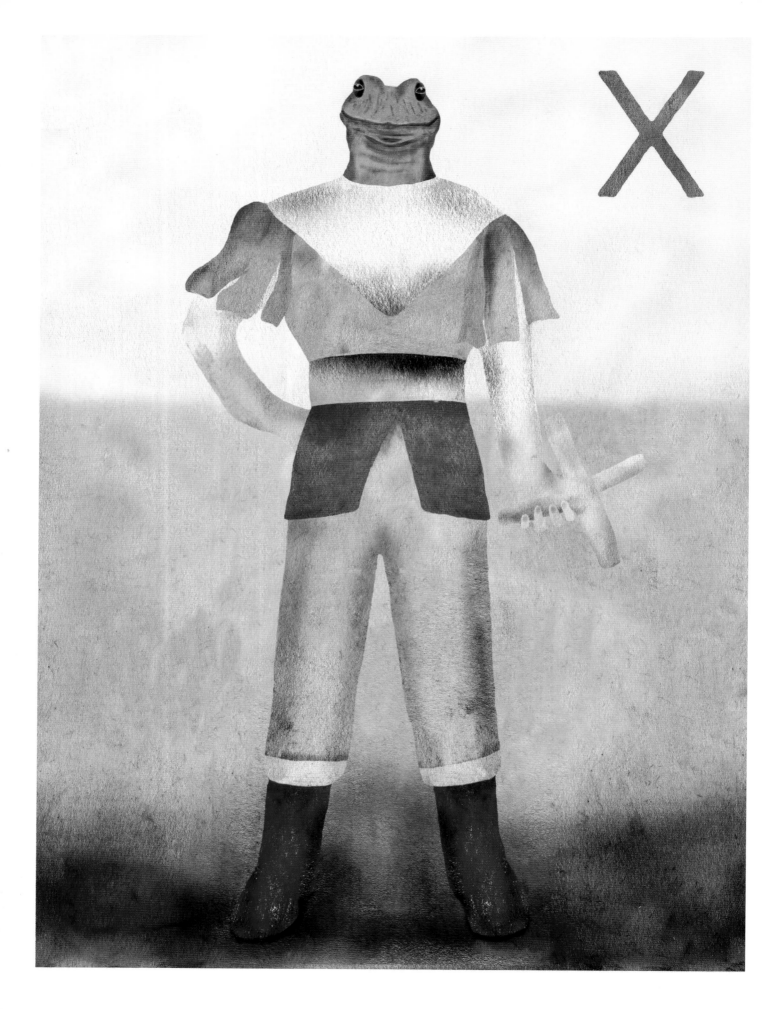

I'm Prince Xavier from Xai-Xai, Mozambique.
I find *The X Factor* exhilarating, X-word puzzles
exciting, and the X chromosome extraordinary.
I'm an expert on xenogenesis and xylography,
but suffer from xerosis. I export X-ray and
Xerox machines to Xian, Xining, Xiangtan,
and Xinjiang, and can express myself in Xibe.
As a xenophile I expect to make expeditions
exploring exotic places such as Xique-Xique,
Xochob, Xylophagou, and Xangongo, and to
exercise my xenoglossia among the Xhosas. My
ex-wife was an excruciatingly exasperating and
exigent Xanthippe, and I'd like to experience
the ecstasy of an exquisite Ximena who will
extol my expertise on the xylophone.

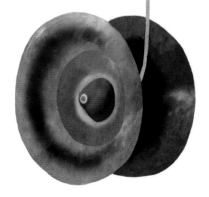

Yo, you young yuppies, I'm Prince Yair, born in Yavne, Israel. You've seen me on YouTube yackety-yacking with Yankees in Yonkers, yachting on the Yangtze and the Yukon, and yodeling in Yarmouth, York, and Yeovil. I eat yams, yogurt, and yummy Yorkshire pudding, and tell yarns about yetis. I sang "Yeah! Yeah! Yeah!" with Yoko Ono, "Yellow Submarine" with Neil Young, and "Yesterday" with The Yardbirds. I yearn for a youthful Yiddisher princess with a Yamaha, and at Yuletide we'll yo-yo under the yew tree till the New Year. Yippee!

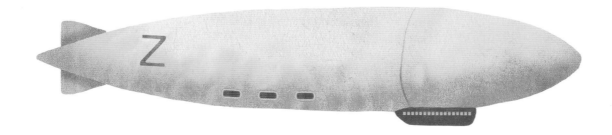

I'm Prince Zwaambi of Zambia,
and I'm full of zeal and zing. I
have a zest for zany hazards such
as zigzagging down the Zambezi
River, zooming over the Zagros
Mountains, or zipping across the
Zuider Zee. I've zapped zebras in
Zaire, zebus in Zambia, and zanders
in Zurich. I've played the zither to
zombies in Zululand, practiced Zen
in New Zealand, zigzagged through
the zoo in Zimbabwe, eaten zucchini
and zabaglione in Zagreb, and done
zilch in Zaragoza. I dream that my
zeppelin, blown by a zillion zephyrs,
will carry my Zenocrate and me to
the zenith of the zodiac.

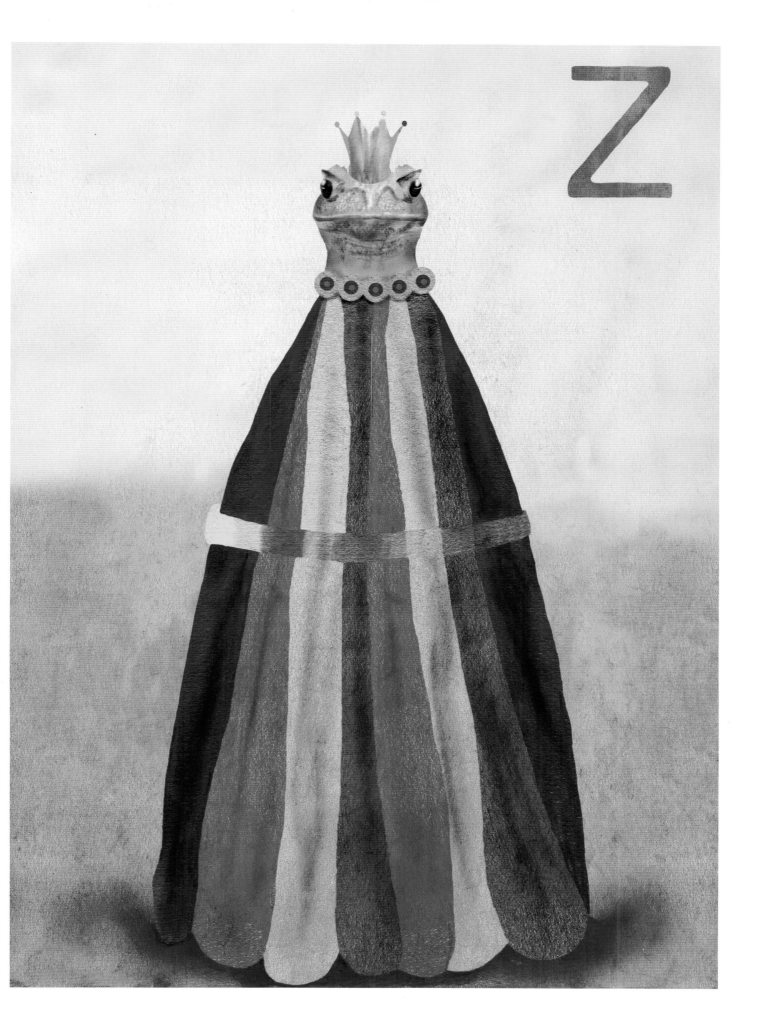

The Princes' Ball has been a great success! Every princess
has found herself a prince. Now they've all gone off on their
honeymoons, blissfully happy in their own special ways.
If only we knew which princes were with which princesses.
Which prince would you have chosen?